Go to Sleep Mom!
Copyright © 2016 Sweet Lemon

sweetlemonbooks.com
maryeakin.com

Time for bed.

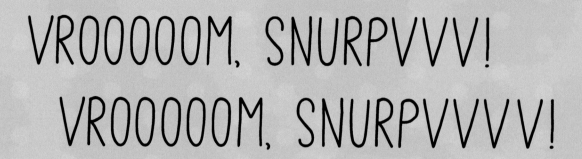

VROOOOOM, SNURPVVVVV!

VI VROOOOOM, SNURPVVVVV!

Shhh, we don't want mom
to know we're out of bed.

What's this?

#2 PACK THE LUNCHES

Hmm, I need a veggie.
What do you think,
popsicle or cupcake?

#3 WASH THE DISHES

We have to be quick.

#4 WASH THE LAUNDRY

Smells good to me.

#6 WASH THE DOG

Why not together?

Now what have you four been up to?

It's all done.
Go to bed mom.

Good night mom.

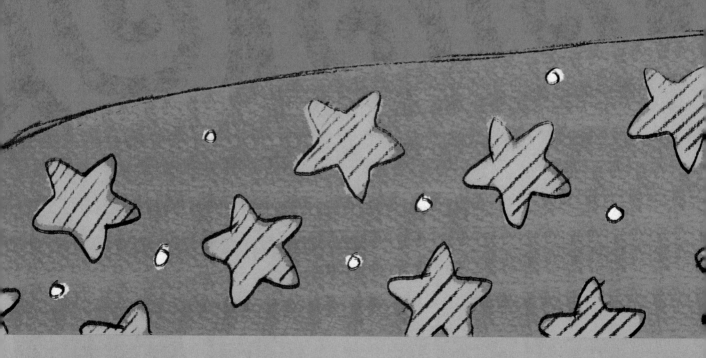

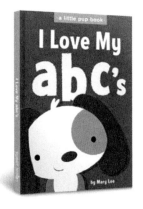

I Love My abc's

SUPER FISH
By Mary Lee

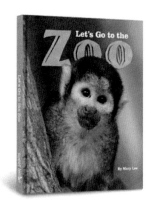

Let's Go to the Zoo

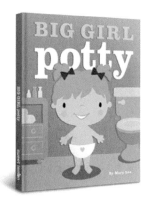

BIG GIRL potty

sweet lemon

Check out more Sweet Lemon Books at
sweetlemonbooks.com

Little Girl Pink

Crazy, Wonderful SCIENCE
By Mary Lee

THE SMARTEST PRINCESS

Why? Because I Love You!
by Mary Lee

Made in the USA
Coppell, TX
07 December 2019